BOOKS BY LAURA (L.A.)MARIANI

Holiday Romance

14 Days to Love Series: Short Sweet Steamy

Parisian Serendipity

Venetian Whispers

Mumbay Surprise

Romeo in Rome

New York Melody

Artic Embrace

Santorini Sunsets

Havana Heat

Barcelona Dreams

Marrakesh Magic

Vienna Waltz

Sydney Sparks

Amsterdam Affair

Cape Town Safari

Box Set

14 Days to Love: Short Sweet Steamy

Twelve Days of Christmas Series

A Partridge in a Pear Tree: Hot Spicy Christmas Novella

Two Turtle Doves: Hot Spicy Christmas Novella

Three French Hens: Hot Spicy Christmas Novella

Four Calling Birds: Hot Spicy Christmas Novella

Five Golden Rings: Hot Spicy Christmas Novella

Six Geese a-Laying: Hot Spicy Christmas Novella

Seven Swans a-Swimming: Hot Spicy Christmas Novella

Eight Maids a-Milking: Hot Spicy Christmas Novella

Nine Ladies Dancing: Hot Spicy Christmas Novella

Ten Lords a-Leaping: Hot Spicy Christmas Novella

Eleven Pipers Piping: Hot Spicy Christmas Novella

Twelve Drummers Drumming: Hot Spicy Christmas Novella

Box Set

Twelve Days of Christmas

Shadowbrook Paranormal Series

A Halloween Romance: Enchanted in Shadowbrook

The Midnight Hour:A Halloween Shadowbrook Romance

Navy Seals Hunks Series

SEALed Hearts

SEALed with a Kiss

SEALed Undercover

SEALed Pursuit

SEALed Love Code

SEALed beyond Duty

The Nine Lives of Gabrielle Series

Gabrielle (prequel/first in series)

For Three She Plays

A New York Adventure

Searching for Goren

Tasting Freedom

For Three She Strays

Paris Toujours Paris

Me Myself and Us

Freedom Over Me

For Three She Stays

London Calling

Back in Your Arms

The Greatest Love

Box Sets

For Three She Plays - Book 1-3

For Three She Strays - Book 4-6

For Three She Stays - Book 7-9

The Nine Lives of Gabrielle Book 1-9 + 3 Bonus stories

Box Set - Italian Edition

Le Nove Vite di Gabrielle: Libri 1-9 + 3 Bonus

A ROYAL ROMANCE TRILOGY

A ROYAL ROMANCE

LAURA (L.A.) MARIANI

A CORONATION
WEEKEND ROMANCE

1

THE VEUVE

Maggie woke up in her plush bed in the Deluxe Suite at the Gilbey, a delightful bar, restaurant town-house offering a five-star bed and breakfast in the heart of Windsor.

She was making a quick pit stop in England to catch up with her old friend Sam before heading toward the Kingdom of Monois to cover the coronation of the new King over the weekend.

All remaining royal families worldwide would be in attendance together with prominent heads of State, a spectacle to behold.

Stretching in the big bed, she couldn't believe how far she had come: her trip was sponsored and fully paid for by major brands for her highly successful and influential blog "The Veuve", feeding the American fascination with all things royals, the pomp and the ceremony.

• • •

Maggie was living the life of her dreams, travelling first class, attending premieres, fashion shows, and a VIP in all major clubs. Who would have thought this was the same podgy shy teenager who once made a living serving tables and cleaning rooms?

She first met Sam at the end of her gap year backpacking through Europe.

England was her last stop before going back home to New York. After seeing the usual touristy places, she finished her year-long trip in Windsor, hoping to satisfy her childhood dream of seeing Queen Elizabeth, a real queen.

She spent a few months there, trying to make enough money to return home. Memories of serving behind the bar at The Reisse were flooding in. Sam was another barmaid there, paying her way through college, working weekend and evening shifts. They clicked immediately and stayed in touch ever since.

The Reisse was a pub in the town of Eton, on the opposite bank of the river Thames from Windsor, connected by a footbridge.

Eton, the home of the notorious all-boys boarding college, possibly the most famous public school in the world, founded by King Henry I, "the chief nurse of England's statesmen", educating generations of British and foreign aristocracy.

. . .

It was at the back of the Reisse that she lost her virginity to a blondish blue-eyed Etonian boy on a drunken night. She could have sworn he was a virgin too.

Maggie and Sam were doing a shift there on a bustling night.

A group of Etonians were gulping down pints and shots; they were loud and bolshy, as they mostly were in her experience. One of them caught her eyes. And she caught his. He kept glancing over, then winking. Then kept coming over to the bar to order more rounds.

Maggie hoped he asked her for more than just drinks. And eventually, he did.

"Can I wait for you when you finish your shift?" he asked.

"You're drunk", she replied.

"Indeed I am. Nevertheless, my dear, I still want to be with you; you are utterly beautiful", slurring his very poshly pronounced words.

"I'll think about it".

. . .

He kept asking, showering her with compliments and buying her drinks.

"You have beautiful eyes", he kept pressing, "and a delightful accent. Where are you from?"

"New York", Maggie answered.

She knew she couldn't play hard to get for much longer but was enjoying the game, for the first time feeling desired. Maggie had always been a tomboy, partly because she grew up with two brothers but mainly because she had always been insecure and uncomfortable with her weight.

His friends teased him whenever he went back and forward to their table; she could see him blushing.

"So endearing," she thought, smiling and feeling flattered.

When Maggie finished her shift, he was right there, waiting. She was thrilled to see him there; it hadn't been just all talk. He pulled her toward him and kissed her. His lips pressed onto hers, his tongue working his way.

"You taste so good", he said, "come ..." he gestured, grabbing her hand while they were making their way to the back of the pub.

. . .

He pushed her against the wall, fondling her breasts. She moaned. He fondled more. She kept moaning. He unbuttoned her blouse and leaned forward to suck her nipples.

"Ah!"

"Sorry", he whispered. "Did I hurt you?"

"A little", Maggie replied.

By now, their jeans were down to their ankles. Although that wasn't exactly how she envisaged she'd lose her virginity, she wanted him. Alcohol was for sure helping lower her barriers, but she couldn't deny she wanted him. Badly.

He was rough and sweet, passionate and clumsy. And quick.

Quick and messy, but she didn't care because he had made her feel wanted, desired and beautiful at a time when she didn't recognise herself as such. She seemed to remember he was good-looking but couldn't quite recall his face.

As he pulled his trousers back up, Maggie noticed a small tattoo on his groin, a yellow rose with something else intertwined that she remembered well.

• • •

"That's cute", she said, thinking it was sweet.

"What is that?" she then asked, pointing.

"It's a C", and he could see Maggie's perplexed look on her face. "It's my mother's initial with a yellow rose, her favourite flower".

"She died not long ago", he added.

"Ah". Now that was creepy.

It didn't matter because she was smitten and falling for him. When they finished recomposing themselves, they walked back to the front of the pub, and there they were, his friends.

"He scored, he scored!!! Hip, hip, hooray! Hip, hip, hooray!!!" they screamed in unison, laughing.

"You owe me twenty quid", he answered, pointing his finger while walking toward them.

"The bet was a tenna", they said.

· · ·

"Ten for the shag, the other ten because she is fat", slurring his words.

Maggie stood there, couldn't believe what she had just heard, tears streaming down her cheeks.

"M, come, they are all pricks, Etonian bastards," said Sam, passing a tissue. She had arrived just in time to hear it all.

Knock knock.

The sound from the door jolted her back.

"Good morning Ms Meddle", said the waitress with a smile on her face. Breakfast was here.

The young girl was standing there, looking at her like transfixed, with a stunned smile.

"Do you want a selfie?" Maggie smiled; this happened to her often. People recognising her

"Oh yes, please", the girl responded enthusiastically.

And so she obliged, glad she had already bathed and put

some clothes on. Then, once she was alone again in her room, she ate her breakfast by the window, smiling.

The humiliation and anger of that night years ago were what she needed to start her new life and dream dreams she had never dared before dreaming.

Gone were the insecurities now and any real or perceived flaws.

"Girl, you look good", she thought, looking at herself in the mirror, happy with what was reflecting at her.

Her skin was glowing and tanned after a two-week trip to Barbados, her long dark hair tousled, her slim figure enhanced by skinny jeans and a simple white shirt and heels.

"Fat my ass, you arrogant prick".

2

THE PRODIGAL SON

"Faster, we need to go faster ... " he could see a car chasing them.

"They are on our tail", the headlight flashing in his rear-view mirror, almost blinding him.

"Stop, stop ..... Noooooooooo".

BANG.

Hupert woke up in a pool of sweat. The nightmares were becoming more vivid, the car crash still haunting him, with more and more memories flashing back each time.

Knock, knock.

* * *

"Mate, are you ok?" his friend Thomas on the other side of the door.

"I'm fine, thanks. I'll be down in a minute", he added.

Hupert was making a quick stop in Eton to visit and pick up his old school friend. After college and military service, he had spent years gallivanting around the world incognito, from Africa to ashrams in India.

Now, it was time to go back home.

His brother was about to become King. Their father's health was failing rapidly and too considerably to carry out the heavy duty of a King and Head of State. Maximilian III of Monois was abdicating to his firstborn, Prince Albert, his brother.

After the death of his mother, his father had become increasingly distant and withdrawn; he stopped even talking about her, Queen Carolina, as to wipe her off his and their memory.

He could not believe how the King and his brother continued allowing press members to cover royal events. The bastards had killed his mother and put him in hospital for months, chasing them like dogs down the road.

. . .

And now, he was about to go back into the folds of the Firm. He couldn't entirely accept or adjust to the fact that Albert was about to be crowned King.

"Why him?" The years in almost solitude, contemplation and meditation had done nothing to diminish the jealousy and annoyance of it.

Albert had benefited from all the privileges of his rank and even found love and happiness with his school sweetheart, Princess Violet, and had two children.

The Kingdom's future was now assured.

Albert looks so much like their father with his dark hair and piercing eyes and so unlike him.

And now he was returning to support his brother and perform his duty as was expected of him as a Prince and forth in line to the throne. Dutifully. Uncomfortably.

But before that, Hupert had to have a last swing at freedom and debauchery with his old friends. At least for a night.

The old gang was getting back together for a night at the Reisse.

• • •

The old pub.

Gosh, he still remembered the last night there before he had to be rushed off Eton because of a security incident.

To be fair, his memory was a bit fuzzy with all the drinking they had been doing. The last year in Eton was a blur altogether; after the tragic death of his mother, he tried to bury his head and feelings in alcohol. Lots of alcohol.

He only just about remembered the lovely and sweet girl behind the bar. She didn't treat him differently than anyone else. He relished that. She had beautiful eyes and a north American accent.

And great tits.

Yep.

Great tits; he remembered those but couldn't quite recollect if they ...

"H, are you coming or what?" Thomas was calling.

"I am ready", he responded. "Let's go".

. . .

And so they went out to meet the others, closely followed by the protection officer, his faithful companion everywhere he went.

3

HAVE WE MET BEFORE?

The Reisse had gone through some renovation; nevertheless, it was still the same old-style country English pub with local beers, wines and good old grub.

It was packed, as always.

The old gang was in their usual corner and had already gone through a few rounds when Hupert and Thomas walked in.

"The prodigal son", they shouted, aware of his travelling and distance from his family.

"Your f***ing Highness", Winston said, waving his hand and with a slight bow of the head.

• • •

"You are such a d***", Hupert answered.

"Oh la la", Thomas almost sang, pointing at the door.

"What a stunner".

H turned and saw what he thought was the most beautiful woman he had ever seen, a vision in jeans and a white shirt. Moreover, he felt warm, fuzzy inside, as if he had known her from before.

"Don't look. Cute guys at three o'clock," Sam said to Maggie.

"One looks a bit Neanderthalish with his fuzzy blonde-reddish beard and long hair".

"Yes, Old Etonians, but cute". Wow, he doesn't look like he belongs, Maggie thought. He was totally not the type of guy she always went for; he looked more rough and ready but handsome nevertheless.

"I know you're going to say it is strange, but he looks familiar".

"It is strange", Sam confirmed, "he is not the type you would know".

. . .

"But the type I could know", she winked.

"Oh yes".

"Hello, ladies", Hupert and Thomas said, greeting them both at the bar.

"Hello back", they answered almost in unison.

"Can we tempt you with a drink?"

"No, thank you. It's just a quiet girl's night out," Maggie said, dying to rip his clothes off but wanting to be chased.

"Have we met before?" Hupert then asked.

'You need to try a better line", she answered.

"I'm serious; you kinda look familiar".

"Nope, I'm sorry".

. . .

They kept looking at each other all evening, and Hupert sent bottle of champagne after bottle of champagne to their table, *Veuve Clicquot*, after seeing them order the first one.

After a while, Maggie went to the bathroom to refresh and top up her lipstick, leaving Sam at their table. When she came out, he was there, waiting.

"Hi".

"Are you going to make me beg?"

"Why not? It seems to come naturally ..." she replied.

"Only because I know what I want when I see it, and I won't stop until I get it, whatever it takes", he said.

"Careful what you wish for; you might get it". How *cliché*; she should have thought of something wittier to reply with.

He came so close that she could almost feel the heat from his cheeks.

"Please ... I am begging you".

"Maybe. Later". And then she left without turning.

4

A KISS IN THE REISSE

Maggie and Sam were having a great time, reminiscing about the old days and catching up on their latest achievements and news.

Samantha was an accomplished barrister specialising in commercial disputes.

"So, are you going to go for it?" she finally asked, dying to know.

"He has something about him besides his rugged handsomeness. He looks almost regal yet vulnerable", Maggie answered, not really answering.

"Crikey! How many glasses of champagne have we had? Clearly too many. I don't know about the vulnerable royal crap, but I'll give it to you, and he is handsome".

. . .

"Sooooo … Are you going for it?" She asked again.

"Perhaps".

"Ok, guys, I'm going to love you and leave you", Hupert said to the old gang.

"Shall I expect you later, H?" Thomas asked.

"Hopefully not", he smiled.

"You have the key, don't forget we are getting picked up for the airport in the morning", Thomas added.

"I won't".

He left the table and walked toward Maggie, the protection officer watching from afar.

"He is coming over", Sam pointed out. "It is now or never".

"I'm sure now is later", he said, looking at her deep in her dark eyes and grabbing her hand.

. . .

He led her toward the back of the pub and the stairs leading to the rooms upstairs.

"Where are we going?"

"I got us a room".

"You are so presumptuous," she said, annoyed but relieved as she didn't fancy a grope in a field at her age.

"I am indeed. Shut up, you know you love it," and then he kissed her, his beard tickling her face. The kiss was long, deep, and passionate.

"You are mine", and then he pulled her on his shoulder with one full sweep and carried her up the stairs.

5

IT IS YOU!

F inally. The room. He turned the key as quickly as he could, wanting to rip her clothes off as soon and as quickly as possible.

They started kissing frantically, hungry and thirsty for each other. He was glad she wanted him as badly as he did her. They were both playing a cat-and-mouse game, chasing and pulling.

The shirts came off, then the jeans. They fell on the floor, clumsy, but it didn't matter. They started there. She climbed on top of him, and began to move her hips, first slowly. Then faster and faster.

"Holy s***", he moaned. Maggie could feel him underneath her, growing harder and harder.

. . .

Maggie felt so powerful and inhibited.
    And, most importantly, in control.

She kissed and licked his chest and bit his nipples, moving down slowly; he squeezed her bum and caressed her intimately between the cheeks.

She grabbed his boxers with her teeth and pulled them down. He lifted his hips as he couldn't wait a minute longer. He wanted them off. Now!

"Wow", she thought, seeing his penis now fully erect.

And it was then that she saw it; surely it couldn't be it. Surely not.

But it was—the same tattoo; a yellow rose with an intertwined C on his groin.

"Why did you stop?" no answer.

"What's wrong?" he lifted his head and saw a horrified and angry look on her face.

"What's wrong?" He repeated.

. . .

"You arrogant ... You, You", pointing her finger, now on her feet, "You Etonian prick".

"What have I done?", wait how does she know?

"You owe me twenty quid", she started imitating his voice and demeanour, "Ten for the shag, ten because she is fat".

And all of a sudden, it came back to him, twenty years ago, at the back of the pub.

Not surely, it can't be her. It must be.

She was screaming at him and gesturing while re-dressing herself at the speed of light.

And then she did the unthinkable: she picked up his clothes, threw them out of the window, and ran out of the room, leaving him there butt naked with nothing he could use as cover.

He got up as quickly as he could, still in shock, frantically looking for his phone when there was a knock at the door.

He opened it sheepishly.

• • •

"Your Royal Highness, is there a problem?" the protection officer was there; thank God for that.

"I need some clothes", he said without explaining.

"Yes, Sir, I'll be back shortly; wait for me here".

"As if I am going to go anywhere like this," he thought, shaking his head.

He needed to find her, but she had vanished, and there wasn't time.

The following day he was leaving Eton and flying back to Monois to attend the banquet before the coronation to welcome all foreign dignitaries.

Maggie ran across the footbridge back into her hotel, tears streaming down her face. All the feelings she had repressed for so long bubbled back up with all her insecurities.

Thankfully there was no time for regrets or mulling over; she had to prepare for the biggest live stream of her life: the coronation of King Albert II.

6

THE SECRET PRINCE

The Coronation Order of Service at St Anne Cathedral.

Their Majesties, The King and The Queen Consort, will arrive at the Cathedral in procession from the Palace, known as 'The King's Procession'.

After the Service, Their Majesties will return to the Palace in a larger ceremonial procession, known as 'The Coronation Procession'.

Other Members of the Royal Family will join their Majesties in this procession.

At the Palace, The King and The Queen Consort, accompanied by Members of the Royal Family, will appear on the balcony to conclude the day's ceremonial events.

Rupert was looking at the official palace's announcement, dreading to meet his family; it had been years since he had seen his father, brother and his beloved grannie, Queen Cecilia.

Fortunately, there was little time for deep discussions between the banquet and the fact that he had to attend rehearsals for the procession and the coronation.

He knew, however, that the time would come sooner or later. But that time was not now.

First, though, the last-minute fitting and check for his ceremonial uniform. He had missed not being in the military, perhaps the only thing he did miss during his travels.

"The beard needs to go", Queen Cecilia declared, saying what the others didn't dare express,

"and a good haircut, too. You need to look like you belong in that uniform".

"Yes, grandmother", he replied, understanding there was no point in arguing.

His father looked frail and tired, leaning on a walking stick whenever he could and when others were not around. His skin was grey and thin, almost translucent.

. . .

His brother, on the other hand, was as handsome as ever. His wife, Princess Violet, soon to be Queen Consort, was making last-minute preparations and chose to incorporate elements into her dress to honour their late mother.

It was thoughtful but also annoying. It was his mother.

Everybody seemed to have continued their lives as if nothing happened, but he couldn't let go and forgive or forget.

Hupert recalls the precise moment he woke up in his hospital bed and was told she had died at the scene. The days that followed were filled with physical pain from physiotherapy and a sense of void and emptiness.

The state funeral was a spectacle; the whole kingdom and half the world had shown up to say goodbye to his beautiful mother, the Hollywood starlet who married the dashing playboy Prince of Monois and then became a Queen, not just on the silver screen, but in real life. Americans especially were obsessed with her.

After some suitable time, he had returned to Eton and thrown himself into parties, drinking and some pills occasionally—anything to numb the pain and not feel.

He tried to remember what had happened, but everything

was a blur for a long time—everything but the black car following them at speed.

And now, he was back for another state event: the new monarch's coronation, the formal investiture with regalia and crowning in the main Cathedral.

His brother was about to become King. So, from tomorrow, Hupert must bow before the King and his wife.

"Dammit".

"H, you good?" Thomas asked. Thomas, the Duke of Monisque, his long-life Etonian friend who had listened to all his gripes and fears for the last twenty years or so.

"I'm good. Let's do this".

On the eve of the Coronation of King Albert II and Queen Violet, the Monois Royal Family was hosting a Reception at the Palace for Foreign Royalty and Heads of State who were in Monois to attend the Coronation. It was also the evening when Hupert was making his official comeback, standing side by side with his family.

"Your Majesty", Hupert greeted King George III of Saint Moncito, a long-distance cousin of his father. The two seemed to try to avoid each other as best they could. Their feud was common knowledge, although nobody knew how or why it started. Nevertheless, duty is duty.

"Nice to see you, Your Highness; glad you are back", he responded.

Hupert nodded.

"You seem distracted", Queen Cecilia whispered.

"A lot to take in", he answered.

"Seems to me more like girl trouble," she said with a wink in her eyes.

Hupert couldn't believe his ears. He had been thinking about her all day and night.

"I have seen that look before. In your father when he met your mother. Something I should know?" she added.

He was about to answer when a flash went off in his face.

"Your Highness, they are doing their job," his protection officer quickly intervened, realising he was about to kick off.

. . .

"They have been invited to cover the events".

He had to leave the room and splash cold water on his face —the sounds of sirens in his ears.

"H … H?" Thomas had followed him into the bathroom with his guard.

"I am good, I am good. For a second, I thought I heard ambulance sirens."

"I just need a minute", he then added.

Commander Philips nodded and made a quick exit. He had to see the King.

"Your Royal Highness",

"Commander".

"The time is near, Sir".

"Thank you, Commander", King Maximilian answered. Hupert was beginning to remember. It won't be long now, and it couldn't have happened at a worse time. He had been dreading this moment for the last twenty years.

· · ·

Maggie had also arrived in Monois to cover the coronation, wanting to focus firmly on her job and trying to soak in the momentous occasion.

The Coronation of His Majesty The King and Her Majesty The Queen Consort will occur at St Anne Cathedral.

As previously announced, the Service will reflect the Monarch's role today and look towards the future while rooted in longstanding traditions and pageantry.

Usually, a coronation would be a symbolic formality and not signify the official beginning of a monarch's reign; *de jure* and *de facto*, the reign would commence from the moment of the preceding monarch's death, maintaining the legal continuity of the monarchy.

But in this case, King Maximilian III was abdicating.

Additionally, all other European monarchies have abandoned coronations favouring inauguration or enthronement ceremonies, making this event even more extraordinary.

Maggie knew she was lucky to be here. She would have loved to be at the reception tonight but wasn't 'official press' and, therefore, not invited to cover.

. . .

She had, however, secured the best place in town tomorrow to watch the procession go by and carry out her live stream.

She was so excited she could barely sleep. Oh yes, and him. The asshole who took her virginity for a bet, and she almost fell for, once again, last night.

"Margaret Meddle: what's wrong with you?" she said sternly to herself.

"Tomorrow is a big day, don't mess up. And who knows? You might even meet your prince charming with all the royals and aristocrats in town."

"Universe, I'm open for some magic in my life", she declared before finally going to bed.

Maggie woke up bright and early; her make-up artist and stylist were in her room helping her getting ready. She couldn't disappoint the brands sponsoring her trip and coverage of the coronation and was making sure she was the perfect brand ambassador.

She had the perfect spot, near the CNN and BBC crews.

. . .

The day he had dreaded was here. Finally, his brother would be King, the job he had prepared for all his life. And now that he had two children, his place in the succession line had gone even further. Hupert was really and truly a spare now.

"Let's get this show on the road", he thought.

The Queen Mother, his Father, brother, and his wife were all taking position so the procession could begin.

Hupert took his place and boarded the armoured royal car.

"Here we go".

The streets were lined up with people four-five deep; they had camped for days waiting.

The Royal family would be the last to arrive in the Cathedral after foreign royals, politicians, and, finally, the soon-to-be King and Queen.

"Your Royal Highness?" said his protection officer sitting in the front seat.

"Yes, Commander?" Hupert answered.

• • •

"You are meant to smile and wave, Sir".

"Oh yes, I forgot."

"It is a glorious day out here, " Maggie told the camera. "The sun is shining, it is warm, and the atmosphere is priceless.

"The procession is about to pass by. But, wait, wait … I can see a royal car arriving."

People started screaming.

A handsome blonde royal was waving to the crowd.

"Prince Hupert, Prince Hupert", young girls were screaming.

He turned his face, and then she saw him. Without the beard and the long hair, but definitely him. In a royal car in full ceremonial regalia.

As he waves around, he saw her too.

"He is a Prince".

7

———

THE TWAIN

The car had arrived in front of the Cathedral.

"Sir"

"Sir, you need to get out of the car".

Hupert was transfixed. She was there, covering the coronation. Perhaps a member of the press, his more dreaded profession.

"Oh yes," Hupert replied.

The door opened, and he stepped out. Cheers and screams left and right. A glance, a smile and a wave.

. . .

And he was in. Hupert took his assigned place and waited for the rest of the procession to arrive. He had to talk to Thomas.

Everything seemed to go so slowly.

A set ritual steeped in history: the Recognition, the Oaths, the Anointing, the Investiture and Crowning, and finally, the Enthroning and Homage.

He had to concentrate and perform his duties, including swearing his allegiance to his brother, the King.

Maggie was trying to remain calm and act like nothing happened whilst interviewing members of the public who were keen royalists.

The prodigal son had returned, Prince Hupert of Monois, soon third in line to the throne.

She had lost her virginity to a Prince—still an asshole, but a royal asshole.

Hupert couldn't wait for the day to be over. There was still the long procession to come and the salute from the balcony, followed by a lunch.

. . .

He had to find a way to reach her. He believed in destiny, and the fact that he met her on his first day back in the same place, the same town, spoke volumes to him. She was special. It was meant to be.

The cameras were following the royal family's every move and expression. Hupert couldn't think of more painful torture.

Smile, wave, and appear interested. More smiling.

The service was over, and as they made their way out of the cathedral, he turned and looked straight into her eyes.

"Sorry", he whispered with an almost imperceptible move of the lips before taking his place in the hundred-year-old royal carriage.

She stared back.

The second ceremonial procession was grander, longer, and more pompous. Hupert had been away so long that he had forgotten the restraint and patience one has to exercise to go through these events.

Hupert couldn't remember her name.

• • •

"Oh God, did I ever ask her?"

The horrified look on her face when she recognised his tattoo told him he had not exactly been a gentleman. His Eton days had not been his best. It's a miracle he managed to finish school and not get arrested in the process.

Hupert didn't want to lose her. She still had the most beautiful tits. Those he remembered well.

Maggie had to continue with her live stream until the end of the day. Guest after guest, interview after interview. Everything was a blur.

"He said sorry", she was thinking. "Did I imagine it?"

"Sorry for what? For having sex with me for a bet? For not telling me he is a Prince?" well, she could understand that one.

"For not at least apologising the days after? Sorry for what?"

The official order of the day was finally coming to an end. Now he had to find her.

. . .

"Commander, I need a favour", he said, approaching his protection officer after the salute from the balcony.

"Yes, Sir".

"Outside the Cathedral, on the right-hand side, there was ...", and before Hupert finished talking, he handed him a piece of paper.

"What is it?" looking perplexed.

"The hotel where Ms Margaret Meddle is staying with her room number".

"How did you ... never mind. Thank you, Philips, thank you".

The Commander nodded.

Maggie was back at her hotel; she had ordered room service, she couldn't bring herself to mingle with people.

Knock knock.

She opened the door, thinking it was her dinner. But it wasn't. It was instead a humongous bunch of flowers.

And then some more flowers and more flowers after that: apology flowers and red roses.

. . .

Lots of red roses.

Her room was now covered with flowers. She had no time to sit down when there was another knock on the door.

"Yes", she said as she opened the door.

"A man desperate to be forgiven by the woman he loves has got all the flowers on sale", he said, standing there with a single red rose in his hand.

She knew then that some magic would enter her life and the twain be made one.

EPILOGUE

The next day, Hupert had invited Maggie to the Palace; the Royal Family was hosting a garden party, this time with no press, only royals and aristocrats from around the world.

H was keen to introduce Maggie to his family and friends and for her to see him in 'his environment'.

"Remember, you need to curtsy in front of my family and everyone at that party.
    Just the first time you greet them".

"What? Do you ..?"

"Yes. Even royals bow and curtsy to the King and Queen— and anyone who outranks me. You'll see, all royals greet each other with a bow or a curtsy".

. . .

"I am an American", she said.

"You are not in America now but meeting the Royal Family", he replied. "That's the way it is, darling".

"You are going to be fine, don't worry, they'll love you", trying to reassure her.

His brother was polite but distant, his wife warmer and more welcoming.

"What a sight for sore eyes", Queen Cecilia proclaimed. "I knew it" Looking at him to say, "See, I knew".

"Grandmother, this Ms Margaret Meddle from New York", Hupert said, introducing her.

He quickly pulled her back as he could see she was going for a hug, trying to signal to curtsy.

"It's quite all right, my dear", she said, " Hupert, I don't bite".

They walked out into the palace garden side by side. "Follow my lead", he whispered.

. . .

So many people he had not seen since childhood were there, including Princess Victoria of Moldof, who used to tease him mercilessly, his once promised one.

"Your Royal Highness", she greeted him with a curtsy.

"Your Royal Highness", he replied with a bow.

"Ms Margaret Meddle", he introduced her.

Maggie curtsied.

"How delightful".

Mwah mwah, and she walked off.

"What was that?" she asked him.

"Don't worry. Victoria doesn't like many people".

"Who is that?" the princess asked Thomas, Duke of Monisque.

. . .

"Hupert's new girl", he replied.

"Mmmm", sipping champagne.

"Victoria … don't be mean", he said.

"I don't know what you mean, Thomas darling".

Overall, the day went smoothly, and Maggie managed to survive it. After supper, they retired to his apartments in the palace.

"Wow" her mouth wide open. "Wow, wow, wow!!!
    This is yours?" she asked.

"It's a royal palace belonging to the Crown and the State. My family's. I use these", he answered.

"Let's go to bed. I've wanted to kiss you all day".

"Just kiss?" she smiled.

He took her in his arms and threw her on the bed.

• • •

"Not quite, my dear. I'm going to f*** you all night like there is no tomorrow".

"Your Hardness, yes, please".

And so he did. They fell asleep wrapped in each other he was still inside her. Until …

"Nooooo ….. "

"H, wake up, wake up. It's a dream," Maggie said, touching his arm.

"I killed her. I killed her", he was shouting.

"It was a nightmare, baby; it is not real", she said, trying to soothe him.

"No, no. I killed my mother. I remember now. I was driving, I killed my mother".

THE WICKED PRINCESS

PROLOGUE

"Nooooo ….." Hupert was screaming at the top of his lungs, sweating profusely.

"Nooooo …".

"H, wake up, wake up. It's a dream," Maggie said, touching his arm. "Wake up," she repeated. He was stone cold and wet, kicking and screaming, lost in his nightmare.

"I killed her. I killed her," he was shouting.

"It is a nightmare, baby; it is not real", she said, trying to soothe him.

"Noooo …".

Bang!

. . .

The door swung open, and Commander Philips appeared at the door with two other protection officers. Maggie barely managed to cover her naked breasts with the bedsheets.

"Your Royal Highness", he said, directed at Hupert.
    "Sorry, Ma'am", removing his glaze.

"No, no. I killed my mother," still dreaming.

"It's all right, Your Highness, it's all right," Philips said while grabbing him from the bed.

"I remember now. I was driving".

"It's a dream," he continued. "Ma'am, we need to take care of His Highness. Do you need anything?" he added.

"No, I am okay, thank you", Maggie responded in shock. And just like that, he was gone.

Maggie waited and waited for him to come back until she fell asleep…
    "Nooooh, I killed my mother …" kept playing in her ear.

. . .

Princess Victoria of Moldof was wandering the palace corridors; she wanted to surprise Hupert. She had decided to sneak into his apartments and rekindle their fling. After all, he couldn't have known that American girl for long; he had just returned.

She wore a long laced négligé over her short, revealing nightgown, her long blond hair loose over her shoulders and a smear of lipgloss.

Doors banging. More noise. Screams.

"What on earth is that?" she thought. As she looked around the corner she saw Commander Philips with other protection officers carrying Hupert out of his quarters.

He seems delirious. "I did it, I did it", he was muttering.

"It was a dream, Your Highness."

Victoria followed them down the corridors right outside King Maximilian's residence in the palace. She wanted to know more but could not go closer. Guards were stationed there.

She could still hear the screams.

• • •

"What did he do?" she thought, curious. "I need to know; it must be important", she muttered as she returned to her room.

King Maximilian had woken up with the noise and was standing there.

"Your Royal Highness, we need to sedate him", he said.

The King nodded.

After Hupert was firmly in bed asleep, Commander Philips briefed him. "The time is near", he then said.

"I'm afraid so, Commander".

1

———

LIKE A PRINCESS

T *antara, tantara …*

Maggie woke up wrapped in the silk bedsheets, the sunshine beaming on her face. She stretched her arms, feeling the bed. It was empty. Hupert was not there. Their clothes were still scattered all over the floor.

Tantara, tantara …

Trumpets sound. She stood at the floor-to-ceiling window, peaking through the heavy-draped curtains.

The pond gardens and its drained, south-facing walled compartments provided shelter for tender exotic plants leading to the privy garden, a quiet space for the monarch's exclusive use, an Italianate-style garden with classical statues on display.

"I can't believe it: I have slept in a Royal Palace," she said. "A real Palace," there were people outside, walking about.

"With a real Prince", still incredulous. The little girl inside her quivering with excitement.

Her thriving and influential blog, "The Veuve", had been feeding the American fascination and her own with all things royals, the pomp and the ceremony. And now this.

But who could have thought a trip to cover the Coronation of King Albert II and Queen Violet of Monois would lead to reuniting with the man she had slept with (and secretly fallen for even if had been a jerk) over twenty years ago?

And he is a Prince. Prince Hupert of Monois.

Maggie was living her childhood dreams.

The next day, he had invited her to the Palace; the Royal Family was hosting a garden party for only royals and aristocrats.

Many had prolonged their stay. And so had she, with a night of unbridled passion and shenanigans.

. . .

"Hupert?" she called out. "Hupert", louder. He was not back yet.

She debated for a while on what to do. Time was passing by; she had work to and needed to get back to her hotel.

Suddenly, the door opened; she grabbed the curtain to cover her naked body.

"Hello, gorgeous", said Prince Hupert, walking into the room with a mischievous look. He was shaved, showered and dressed in smart casual clothes.

"Hi", she replied with a beaming smile. She wanted to ask him about the previous night, where did he go? Why didn't he come back? But instead, she just said,

"I need to go."

"Oh no, you don't".

"I REALLY need to go".

"No can do", he replied, grabbing her over his shoulder and throwing her back in the bed.

"What are you doing?"

· · ·

"I want to ravish every inch of your body".

Maggie did not know if to feel annoyed by his neanderthal behaviour or flattered by his passion.
    "I need to .."

"Later", kissing her voraciously.

They spend the rest of the morning in bed.

Things moved quickly from there. Prince Hupert invited Maggie to accompany him to a secluded cottage in the depths of the Royal land, a kind of official first date (considering they didn't have one in the first place).

"Darling, come and join me", he said, "There we can be by ourselves and make sure that we have a chance to get to know each other."

Maggie was hesitant. She only had a few days left in Monois before returning to New York. She still had commitments to fulfil.

"Everything feels so right and so normal with you," he added, trying to break down her resistance.

· · ·

"I have some work that I need to finish", she said, knowing perfectly well she could not refuse him.

"We do have Wifi in the Kingdom, you know?" he said, smiling.

Maggie nodded.

Suddenly, it hit him,
    "This girl, this woman is amazing, is everything I've been looking for, and she's so comfortable and relaxed in my company. I can't lose her".

This was the first time they'd spent real time together, and Hupert wanted to show her all his favourite places. More importantly, he wanted to show her what the future could hold.

Days went by, walking, cooking together, talking and visiting the Kingdom incognito.

The attraction for each other growing with each minute passing by. But so were his nightmares. Each day longer and more frightening. Each day more vivid.

Maggie was dying to ask but didn't dare.

• • •

He knew one day he would remember it all but, right now, was too scared to find out.

"Tomorrow", Hupert whispered.

"Yes?" she replied.

"You are leaving", he said, sighting.

"Yes, New York is home", Maggie replied.

"I am going to miss you. I'll visit soon if you want me", he added.

"Of course. And I'll miss you too".

They made love all night, feasting on each other like hibernating creatures feast on the autumn harvest before entering the hibernaculum.

2

BACK TO REALITY

The taxi ride to the airport seemed endless. She sauntered through the gate, her feet as heavy as her heart. She slept all the way, feeling exhausted.

New York was as beautiful and as busy as ever. And so was her schedule. Thankfully.

She had allowed herself to be swept off her feet into a dream. But surely, she is no Princess, right? She is a modern working woman.

Maggie loved her life. She had never thought what a relationship with a Royal would mean, it had always only been a fantasy, a childhood fantasy.

"This cannot be real", she thought.

. . .

She was independent, used to looking after herself and with high hopes and ambitions. Her cover of the Coronation had gone viral, and views had skyrocketed. She was hot property now more than ever.

The Statue of Liberty was standing glorious in the afternoon sun. Her American Dream still very much alive.

But despite her cry for independence she missed her Prince.

"I wonder what is he doing? Does he miss me?"

Prince Hupert was meeting with his brother, the new King, and his secretary to discuss the royal calendar and his duties as a working royal supporting the monarch.

School openings, hospitals, old pensioners' homes, veterans'. The list went on and on as if he had never been away. He was missing her already and could not stop thinking about her.

"Hupert?" King Albert said. "Are we boring you?"

"Sorry, your Highness, of course not. I am just a little tired", Hupert jolted back to reality.

"Thank you, Sir Clinton", the King then said. "That would be all."

The royal secretary left the room, leaving them alone for the first time since his return.

"It's nice to have you back, H, " he said.

"It feels right to be back. Father looks tired", Hupert replied.

"Yes. *Papa* has been carrying the weight of the world on his shoulders", the monarch said. "More and more so lately. Something is worrying him deeply".

Hupert nodded, wondering if it had anything to do with him. "It must", he was thinking.

"On a lighter note, Victoria has been asking about you when you were away", King Albert noted with a wink.

"Your Highness!?!" Hupert said with an incredulous expression.

"She is still in the Palace and will be at dinner with us tonight".

"I have a girlfriend", Hupert followed up.

• • •

"Girlfriend? You just met her", the King said incredulously. Hupert could feel his anger rising.

"Anyhow", moving on swiftly, "she is with us for supper. Be polite. *Papa* loves her, and she is one of us".

"What does he mean by one of us? Was that a dig at Maggie?" Hupert was thinking, getting angrier.

"Will do, Your Highness", he said instead.
     "Hupert, common. Don't be a child", the King said as he was leaving the room.

Princess Victoria got ready for dinner with extra care. She was eager to show she was part of the family, and at the same time, she wanted to seduce him. It worked before, and it would again. She was sure.

And there was a mystery to solve. What had Hupert done that he had to be carried into his father's rooms in the middle of the night?

Victoria was also determined to find out one way or another.

The entire Royal family of Monois was present for the semi-official dinner, and a few of the remaining royal guests from the Coronation, including King George III of Saint Mocito, a long-distance cousin of the former King Maximilian, Princess Victoria of Moldof and Thomas, Duke of Monisque, Hupert's old Etonian friend.

Everyone was relaxed, as relaxed as royals get, and exchanging pleasantries. Victoria sat strategically between Hupert and the King Father, playing footsie with one and charming the other.

"Daa-arling? How are you feeling now?" she asked Hupert suddenly.

"Very well, thank you", he answered, perplexed.

"Are you sure? You seemed pretty out of it the other night", she continued.

"Don't worry, your secret is safe with me", Victoria added with a wink softly in Hupert's ear but loud enough for his father to hear.

Hupert's cheeks were bright red, his palms sweating. King Maximillian coughed.

"No secret, Victoria", he responded.

. . .

"Sure, daa-arling." She knew she had touched a nerve with both.

King Albert was staring from across the table, wondering what she was talking about, worried about the look on his father's face.

After dinner, everyone moved into the reading room for coffee and vintage liqueur. King Maximillian and King George III of Mocito left the others for a private meeting.

After an hour or so, they all retired to their rooms.

Hupert could not wait to FaceTime Maggie. Seeing her face and hearing her voice was the highlight of his days. He dreaded going to sleep, the nightmares haunting him.

Knock knock

Hupert was about to shower when someone knocked at the door.

"Thomas, my friend, we can talk tomorrow," he thought. But it wasn't him.

"*Surprise!!*" Victoria was there instead in her *neglige,*

throwing herself at him, *"Muah muah, smack …"* trying to kiss him.

"Victoria, what are you doing here?" pushing her away.

"You have been utterly impossible daa-arling. I want my goodnight kiss".

"You had too much to drink, Victoria. Time for bed", he replied.

"Yes, please", Victoria said enthusiastically.

"Your bed, not mine".

"One-night Hupert".

"I am seeing someone; go to bed. Good night, Victoria", and he closed the door.

Victoria walked away more determined than ever. Nobody rejects her. Not even a Prince.

Buzz buzz

. . .

"Hi baby", Hupert said, lying butt naked on the bed.

"Hi. OMG, you are naked", she said. Maggie had fortunately ran outside the coffee shop to answer.

"Nothing you haven't seen before. Did you miss me?" Hupert answered with a big cheeky smile.

"Baby, it's early over here; I'm out and about, you know? Working," she replied a bit annoyed.

"Oops! I was so looking forward to talking to you ... and more *wink wink*".

"Perhaps we can schedule our calls so I am prepared?" Maggie went on.

"Am I disturbing you? Is there someone with you?" He was starting to feel anxious now.

"No, no. We just can't be that careless when I am out in public. Especially with you naked. That is for my eyes only!" She answered, flashing a big smile.

"Okay, point taken. I am going to be busy with my duties, you know, The Firm".

• • •

"OK".

"Miss you", he added.

"Miss you too".

"He misses me", she thought skipping back inside the coffee shop like a school girl.

Texts, phone calls and FaceTime sex became their reality, snatching any time they could in between everyday life.

A long weekend away here and there - New York, Monois, Monois, New York.

A trip to Norway, their first holiday together. Hupert planned the romantic getaway so that the two could catch the Northern Lights. He wanted to make it as fairy-tale and memorable as possible.

Anything and everything for Maggie.

3

PAP-PAP-ARAZZI

Hupert and Maggie avoided the media and were not seen in public together for quite some time. However, after a month of being incognito, the news leaked:

Prince Hupert was dating an American blogger, Margaret Meddle.

A servant tip led to tabloids discovering their relationship.

When the story broke, the prince was with Maggie in New York, her home. His assistant contacted him, informing him their relationship would be "front-story news" and the media would soon ambush them.

Monois!Online

RELEASED PHOTOS REVEAL THE PRINCE WEARING A BASEBALL CAP AND CARRYING A LARGE DUFFLE BAG WHILE ENTERING MEDDLE'S BUILDING.

. . .

Monois Express
PRINCE HUPERT IS "HAPPIER THAN HE'S BEEN FOR MANY YEARS"
AND "BESOTTED" WITH MEDDLE.
IS SHE WITH HIM OR THE KINGDOM?

Maggie was unprepared for the onslaught of attention even though she was in the public eye and was a content creator. Still, little could have equipped her for what was to come.

Paparazzi tried to break into her home and go through her trash; money was offered to her friends and exes for stories.

Her life under scrutiny.

The press continued reporting on them, and the coverage wasn't always pleasant. She tried her hardest to tune out the noise.

The Daily Monois
BREAKING NEWS
A SOURCE REVEALS MS. MEDDLE IS OUT FOR REVENGE - PRINCE
HUPERT, THE LOVER WHO TOOK HER VIRGINITY.

"My God, how do they know this?" Maggie said, crying.

She became paranoid, doubting who she could trust. Including Sam, her long-life friend.

"I swear Maggie. It wasn't me. I never even answer their call". Sam pleaded. "There was a group of his friends outside The Reisse, remember?" More pleading. "And people coming out of the pub".

"Yes, sure". Maggie replied coldly.

Maggie was sure people were "out to bring her down".

Monois Express
EX-LOVER SAYS, "SHE ALWAYS WANTED TO BAG A PRINCE";
THE REAL STORY OF A SOCIAL CLIMBER.

Hupert completely flipped over the story.

Who had betrayed him? Surely not Thomas. Who then?

He feared history repeating itself. His beloved mother, the Hollywood starlet who married the dashing playboy Prince of Monois and then became a Queen, was haunted to her death by paparazzi. Hupert could not allow this to happen to Maggie.

He had to do something.

4

———

FROM THE OFFICE OF PRINCE HUPERT

B*uzz buzz*

Her friend Sam had texted her, "Check Twitter." She said, "Now! #theprinceandthepauper thread".

Maggie checked her phone. Sam was still trying despite Maggie's cold shoulder.

"Oh, My God! What has he done?"

Prince Hupert of Monois had issued a glaring statement confirming their relationship.

Twitter @PrinceHupertofMonois_CommunicationOffice

"Prince Hupert recognises the warmth extended to him by the public since he was young. He feels fortunate to have so much support and knows he has led a privileged life.

He also understands the considerable interest in his personal life. Prince Hupert, however, has never been comfortable with this. Still, he has endeavoured to grow a thick exterior about the media interest that comes with his privilege and never taken formal action on the periodic publication of made-up stories written about him.

But the past week has seen a line crossed: his girlfriend, Margaret Meddle, has been subjected to unspeakable harassment. This has been in part public - smeared on the front page of a nationwide newspaper and the blatant sexism of social media trolls and web piece commentaries. Some other has been hidden from the public - the stabs of correspondents and photographers to gain unlawful entry to her home and the calls to police that followed; the considerable bribes offered by papers to her ex-boyfriends; the pursuit of almost every friend, co-worker, and loved one in her life.

Prince Hupert is worried about Ms. Meddle's safety. He is profoundly aggrieved that he has not been able to safeguard her. It is not right that a month into a relationship with him, Ms Meddle should be subject to such abuse. He knows newscasters will say this is 'the price she has to pay' and that 'she should know how the press and social media work'. He vehemently disagrees. It is their life, not a game.

He has asked to release this statement, hoping those in the press pushing this story can pause and deliberate before further damage occurs. He knows it is uncommon to express this. Still, he wishes that people will comprehend why he has felt it essential to speak publicly."

"I can't believe he has done that!" she texted back. "He didn't even ask me if it was ok".

"He just wants to protect you", Sam replied.

"I can look after myself; I don't need a man to look after me", Maggie continued, the feminist in her furious. The alpha-male part of his character was beginning to get on her nerves.

"Try to see it from his perspective".

"I'm going to be attacked even more now".

"Calm down", Sam added to reassure her. But she was boiling over the statement.

Ring ring

"Hello beautiful", he answered immediately, proud of what he had done.

"How could you?" Her voice shaking.

• • •

"What's wrong?"

"What do you mean 'What's wrong?' Your statement", she replied.

"Baby, I did it for you. For us."

"But, but…"

"I love you. I am in love with you. This is very real for me", he professed staring in her eyes.

"Tell me this is real for you too", he asked her.

"It is."

"You are my princess. It's my job to protect you".

"They are out to get me. Us", she whispered, crying.
   He then he was sure he had made the right decision.

"It's us against the world baby. Us against the world" he reassured.

• • •

Staff at the Palace were surprised by the overtly emotional nature of the statement. Moreover, King Albert had not approved the Prince's message before publication and was furious.

King Maximilian, instead, was terrified this could precipitate events and scandal in the Kingdom.

5

THE PROMISED ONE

Victoria was revelling in reading the front page news.

The Daily Monois
Breaking News
A SOURCE REVEALS MS. MEDDLE IS OUT FOR REVENGE - PRINCE
HUPERT, THE LOVER WHO TOOK HER VIRGINITY.

She smiled. Her trip to Eton and meeting up with Winston had been well worth it.

Monois Express
EX-LOVER SAYS,
"SHE ALWAYS WANTED TO BAG A PRINCE";
THE REAL STORY OF A SOCIAL CLIMBER.

"He is going to come to his senses now. This nonsense had to stop." Victoria was sure her tactics would work. He would feel betrayed, get angry, smash some things like he usually did, and she would be there to console him. Victoria always knew how to play him around her little finger, mentally and sexually.

And if that didn't work, there was always plan B.

"Yes, he will be back. I am the promised one, after all", she smiled.

Her mobile phone was blowing up with messages and voicemails.

"What is going on?"

____

Winston - have you checked Twitter?

____

____

Thomas - Victoria, stay calm

____

"What?".

. . .

And then she saw it—Hupert's statement.

… But the past week has seen a line crossed: his girlfriend, Margaret Meddle, has been subjected to unspeakable harassment. …

Prince Hupert is worried about Ms. Meddle's safety. He is profoundly aggrieved that he has not been able to safeguard her.

Crash! Bang!

There it went, the Ming vase against the wall.

Aaaaaaah!!!

She couldn't believe he had released that statement.

"Ok then. Plan B".

"Your Highness", the royal secretary said. "Princess Victoria of Moldof is requesting a private hearing at your convenience".

. . .

King Maximilian had been expecting this since the dinner. Victoria, such a lovely girl, didn't know the meaning of the word 'no'.

"Yes, sure. Please look at my calendar and find a suitable time," he knew that ignoring her would not make her go away.

"Yes, Sir".

Victoria was surprised how quickly she could get an audience.

"He must be worried", she thought smiling.

"Your Royal Highness, thank you for receiving me at such short notice", Victoria curtsied.

"It is always a pleasure to see you, my dear. What can I do for you?" King Maximilian was dreading her answer.

"Your Highness. Our Kingdoms, Yours and my father's, have always been allies. Friends".

"Indeed, Victoria, indeed".

" Intertwined for centuries", *hem hem.*

• • •

"The two of you always talked about forging a greater alliance, one that comes with blood," she cleared her throat further.

"With marriage".

"Prince Hupert and I were once promised to each other".

"I gather you have seen the statement", he replied.

"I did. I must admit I was extremely disappointed".

"What can I do Victoria? We are not in the 19th century any longer. I can't force him," he added.

"Well, Your Highness",

Ahem hem

"I am sure you have far more influence than you think". She paused.

"There is also the small matter of the Treaty between our two Kingdoms", Victoria continued. "And you can be assured that Hupert's secret, your secret, is safe with me."

She then added quickly. Victoria was throwing everything at it.

A flash of unrepressed anger flickered across the King's eyes. Victoria wondered if she had gone too far.

"It has been nice to see you Victoria. I'm tired now", and she was dismissed. The meeting had come to a close.

"The time has come," he thought. "But first his son Albert, the King, needs to know".

And for the first time in over twenty years, tears started streaming down his cheeks in what seemed an ever ending flow.

6

___

DOWN THE RABBIT HOLE

"Hupert, stop! Please stop!" his mother pleaded while running after him.

King Maximilian III stood there petrified. His worst nightmare was coming through.

"Leave me alone, mother". He replied. He had to get away. What began as a surprise return from Eton had quickly turned into a disaster.

"Darling, you misunderstood", she continued. "Please stop, let's talk about it!"

"There is nothing to talk about. I heard you perfectly", he shouted. "Now it all makes sense! How could you do that?" He said, running towards the car, he had to get away.

. . .

"You can't drive, not like this. You had too much to drink, you are upset".

"Get away from me", he replied, starting the engine.

Queen Carolina barely got into the car before he took off.

The King in the meantime had alerted Commander Philips who had jumped into a protection car to follow them. They were going too fast; the road was dangerous.

"Slow down, you are going too fast", his mother pleaded. "Slow down".

Hupert was in shock, angry; his ears were still playing his parents' fight, the harsh words, his mother's secret.

"Stop, please stop!"

HAAAAAAH

The car swerved off the road down the cliff. Tumble, tumble.

Bang! Crash!

. . .

The airbag blew up in his face.

Haaahh Ugh

"Mother, mother, are you ok?" Hupert turned his head to find an empty seat, the door half hanging on the hinges.

Squeak screech CLOMP CLOMP

"Mother …… where are you?"

"Your Highness, your Highness", Commander Philips was shouting. "Stay with me, Your Highness", trying to districate him from the jumbled car.

"My Mother …".

Commander Philips looked up to see the other protection officers shaking their heads. Queen Carolina was dead.

"Noooo!" the screams woke Maggie up.

"I killed her. I was driving", Hupert jumped off his bed, sweating and shaking.

. . .

"They all know it", he said "They all know it". She cradled him in her arms. He was crying unconsolably , his past unravelling in front of him.

KNOCK KNOCK

"Your Highness", Philips was banging at the door. "Your Highness, are you all right?".

Maggie opened the door, her brown eyes swelling up with tears
    "He is there", pointing. "And no, he is not all right!".

"Your…"

"Don't! Don't try to tell me it was just a nightmare. You know better. I know better now", Hupert screamed.

"I want to speak with my father".

"Very well, Sir", and exited the room.

"Baby it's going to be okay. It is out now", Maggie said, holding his face in her hands, wiping his tears.

"No yet. There is something else I need to know".

7

A FATHER'S LOVE

Commander Philips escorted Hupert to see King Maximilian.

"Your Royal Highness, Prince Hupert is here", he announced.

"Very well, Commander, thank you". The King responded.

"Father, I know. I k-n-o-w!", Hupert said.

"What do you know, Son?" King Maximilian replied, just to be sure.

"I know I was driving. I killed Mother".

• • •

"I see," with a heavy sigh of relief. "You didn't kill her. It was an accident. A tragic car accident, that's all".

"No, Father. I was speeding. I had too much to drink. She begged me to slow down. She begged me to stop, but I didn't listen."
Tears started streaming down his cheeks.

"It's my fault".

"Son, it was an accident".

"Why didn't you tell me? You, commander Philips, Albert …" Hupert continued.

"No, not Albert. He never knew. He does not know", King Maximilian added.

"Why didn't you tell me?" Hupert asked him.

"You were in a coma for a few days, and when you woke up, you had lost your memory. I thought it was a blessing in disguise. I prayed this day never come. I know how much you loved her", his eyes tearing up.
"I couldn't do that to you. I couldn't do that to us as a family!".

. . .

"All those years, I thought the paparazzi pushed us off the road."

"I know".

Hupert hesitated. There was something else.

"You almost withdrew from me and Albert was different …

"You are not the only one who lost a loved one that day. We all did. Sorry, I was not there for you as you needed. My grief …", tears came rushing down.

"And I took her from you".

"No, Son, it's not …".

"I know. I heard you fighting. I heard Mother telling you …" Hupert could not bear to say.

"What did you hear?" King Maximilian asked.

"That … I … am not your son", his voice trembling.

"Your mother was angry, we were fighting …"

· · ·

"Don't lie to me, please. No more lies," Hupert pleaded.

"I have always known since you were a baby. It was not a surprise. I have raised you as my son. You are my son", with open arms.

"You are my son", he repeated.

Hupert hugged his father as he had never before. A long warm embrace.

"We need to call Albert", King Maximilian added. "He needs to know before others tell him".

Hupert looked at his Father with a puzzled look.

"It's a long story. Plus there is a small matter of your statement still to discuss".

"Ah, that! Yes …" Hupert said sheepishly. "I love her".

"I gathered that. Does she love you?", and as he saw his son was losing his temper, he added "Hey I have to ask. Royal life is a commitment to serving your subjects. No complaining. It looks glamours, it really isn't. Your mother had trouble adjusting too", he said with a sad look.

. . .

Hupert wondered if he was referring to her betrayal? Was he scared it would happen to him too?

"I'm sure. I want to spend the rest of my life with her".

"You better make sure she says 'Yes' before we plan a course of action", the King said.

"Uh?"

"Treaties and Kingdoms, Son. Treaties and Kingdoms".

8

———

EVER MORE, EVER AFTER

aggie was waiting anxiously for his return. He had gone for ages. She was worried for him: covering up his emotions for so long and the accident's trauma negatively affected his mental and emotional health.

She was sure he didn't kill his mother. It's probably just the survivor's guilt.

And he said there was more …

"Hi", he said.

"Hi back", Maggie replied, smiling. "How did it go?"

"Better than I expected", he answered.

"Do you want to talk about it?" she asked.

• • •

His father had warned him not to talk about it openly for fear of the repercussions on his brother, his mother's reputation, and the stability of the Kingdom.

The Family had to agree first on the course of action.

But Hupert could not hide from her after all he had put her through.

Knowing what happened didn't alleviate the pain but made everything clear on what his priority was. Maggie.

Everything else did not matter.
    And so he told her.

The car accident, the paternity.

"Oh, my God. Are you all right? How are you feeling now?" she knew it sounded banal but it was all she could muster right now.

And there was more.

A Treaty between Moldof and Monois could jeopardise the security of the Kingdom if he didn't marry the Princess of Moldof.
    He was looking deeply into her eyes when he said it.

· · ·

"Do you mean ….?" she couldn't believe it. Who does that?

"Yes, the Kingdom's fate could rest on the marriage".

She stood up crying. "Ok, this is it then! It was nice until it lasted," she thought, walking away from him.

"Baby?" Hupert said, "Baby, look at me!"

As she turned around, she saw him, on one knee, holding a small red velvet box with the most humongous, gorgeous antique diamond ring.

"Marry me", and smiled.

"But, … the Kingdom …"

"The two of us. Just the two of us. Ever more, ever after. That is all the matter", he responded.

"So???"

"YES, YES, YES", unashamedly unapologetically yes.

THE LOST KINGDOM

1

A FAMILY AFFAIR

"YES, YES, YES", Maggie said, unashamedly unapologetically yes.

Hupert was still on his knee, crying. After the nightmares, a ray of sunshine, a chance for happiness.

"The two of us. Just the two of us. Ever more, ever after. It's all that matters", he repeated.

"Just the two of us", Maggie said, "and a couple of Kingdoms", smiling between the tears.

And soon it would be time to face the music …

"Treaties and Kingdoms", his father said.

"Treaties and Kingdoms", wondering what he meant.

King Maximilian had called an emergency meeting with his mother, Queen Cecilia, his sons, King Albert and Prince Hupert and was waiting anxiously for everyone to arrive.

After all this time, the truth was about to come to light. He had hoped to have more time.

Queen Cecilia was the first to arrive. Followed by Albert and then, finally, Hupert.

"Father, what is that couldn't wait?" King Albert asked.

"The Moldof-Monoisque Treaty of 1848 is the basis of the relationship between the Kingdom of Moldof and Monois. The treaty defines Monois's independent status and sovereignty and the House of Grindsor's succession rights. Our house".

King Maximillian could see the lost look on their faces.

"The 1848 Treaty recognised the sovereignty of Monois. Previously, Monois had been a protectorate of the Austro-Hungarian Empire under the Treaty of Vienna.

•   •   •

At the time, my grandfather had no legitimate children, and the possibility of his French cousins, the dukes of Saint-German, succeeding in the future to the throne was unacceptable to Moldof.

There was pressure for Monois to ratify treaty provisions that would empower Moldof to prevent such an occurrence and unsuitable marriages.

Article 23c of the treaty stipulated that the Moldof and Monois governments must agree upon foreign policy measures, and Article 23d refers explicitly to vetting unsuitable marriages concerning Monois.

A material breach of the treaty by one of the parties entitles the other to invoke the breach as a ground for terminating the treaty or pay damages to the non-breaching party. This would mean that either our sovereignty is under question or that Monois must concede the districts of Montona and Roquebrille-Martin to Moldof, a considerable part of the Kingdom. Neither are viable options".

"As you know, Albert", King Maximilian continued, "we have been negotiating a new Treaty for the last few years concerning issues of sovereignty raised by the revision of our constitution in 2018.

Under those constitutional revisions, although only a born member of the Grindsor line may now wear the Crown, Monois assumed the unilateral prerogative to alter the order of succession and the Kingdom's independence is explicitly secured. The new Treaty would resolve the concerns that under the 1848 treaty, dynastic acts affecting the line required Moldof's consent.

Unfortunately, these changes have not yet been ratified by Moldof under the new Treaty", he finished.

"Father," said Albert impatiently, "it is a 150-year-old treaty. We have been negotiating for months. What is the rush for this meeting?"

Hupert understood now.

"Victoria came to see me to invoke Moldof's rights under the Treaty."

King Albert knew he couldn't possibly be talking about him, turned around, looked at Hupert and said, "I guess congratulations are in order, little brother", with a smile, knowing what Victoria had always wanted.

"I have proposed to Maggie," Hupert blurted out, "and she said 'Yes'".

"You did what? You barely know her."

· · ·

Hupert stood up, angry.

"Boys, we need to focus, stop squabbling", Queen Cecilia intervened, looking at her frail son and his air of despair.

"Victoria has enormous influence over her father. He adores her,' she continued.

"Victoria is also threatening something else," King Maximilian hesitated, knowing the worst was yet to come.

Hupert was now terrified, his palms sweating.

"She is threatening to reveal our secrets", he whispered.

"We haven't got secrets," Albert said with conviction.

"She is probably bluffing, but we better be sure", King Maximilian continued.

"Father", Albert interrupted, "Father, we haven't got any secrets, right?"

"Father?"

• • •

King Maximilian trembled, nervously clinging to his chair.

"Father?"

"It was me," Hupert blurted out.

Albert turned his head slowly …

"I was driving, I lost control, it was me driving", Hupert said sobbing. "Not mother".

"I came back from Eton early after a night out with my friends, and I heard ma and pa fighting. Ma said something that shocked me", the words came as running out of his mouth.
 "I was angry, so angry and I ran to the car".

Albert was incredulous.

"She came after me. I told her to leave me alone. She followed me and jumped in the car with me", Hupert went on.

'I was driving fast", *hem hem,* he cleared his throat, "and I lost control", sobbing.

.   .   .

"And you couldn't stop her …"said Albert, now standing.

"Boys, stop ", Queen Cecilia stood between them. She had kept surprisingly calm amongst the revelations.

"What could you have possibly heard that was so upsetting? Always the hotheaded brother", he continued screaming.

King Maximilian sat silently, shaking his head, his world crashing down around him.

"I am not a Grindsor ", Hupert answered, " I am a b-a-s-t-a-r-d", his lip quivering.

The screams stopped. Minutes went by that seemed like hours.

"You are family", Queen Cecilia quickly said, "We are family and we have a Kingdom to protect. We owe it to our people. Whatever she thinks she knows, it does not matter. We need to take care of it".

King Albert dropped on a chair, the future of his Kingdom now at risk.

· · ·

"No matter what", Queen Cecilia continued, "We are family".

"Come Hupert, come with me", she said. "Your father and the King need to talk now", she took his arm and leaned on him and started to walk.

"But ...", Hupert started.

"Not now, come with me".

2

SOMETIMES LOVE HURTS

Queen Cecilia took Hupert out of the room. She could see he was struggling to cope with his guilt; he could feel the pain in every bone and muscle in his body. But, at the same time, he was raging with anger.

He wanted to smash things and scream. Queen Cecilia knew him well.

Commander Philips had been waiting outside.

"Commander, please make sure no one disturbs my son and the King. They'll be some time".

"Yes, Ma'am", he responded.

. . .

"We are going to my quarters", as to address his puzzled look.

He nodded.

"Why did she have an affair? Was she planning to leave his father? Who is the other man? Who is my 'real' father?" questions playing havoc with his mind.

He wanted answers.

"Gan-Gan, I need to know!" he said, using his affectionate nickname for the Queen Mother.

"I know, my child", she replied with a sweet smile.

"Can I still call you Gan-Gan?" he then asked tentatively.

"Don't you dare stop", she said emphatically.

"Form the moment I saw you, you were and always will be my grandson".

"Gan-Gan, you were very calm ..." Hupert added, "About everything".

. . .

"My darling Hupert, do you think there is anything that happens in the Kingdom that I do not know?"

"You knew???" he asked, surprised.

"Sit down, my child", she said as she called for tea.

"The Kingdom, our people and our family are the most important thing. The Institution. The people count on us for direction, stability and continuity with our past. We cannot let them down", she started.

"No matter what, we must keep united", she continued, looking at his puzzled face.

"When your mother died ..."

"I killed her."

"Stop", gently putting her index finger on his lips, "Stop saying that. It was an accident."

"The Kingdom was in mourning. My son, the King, was distraught, and my two lovely boys, you and Albert, had just lost their mother".

. . .

The servants entered the room with tea and fresh pastries.

"That's all, thank you", the Queen Mother said, dismissing them quickly.

He started to pour the warm, fragrant tea into her cup. He wanted to ask many questions, but he knew she would get there in her own time.

"You hid it so well", he blurted out suddenly.

"Pardon?" she looked at him perplexed.

"You must have hated her. It did not show", Hupert replied.

"I never hated her", she paused to sip her tea, "I was initially angry for her indiscretion, for hurting my son", *sip sip*.

"But I understood. Your mother was young, beautiful and used to a carefree life. Suddenly, she became Queen. Playing one on a silver screen is not the same as Being one", she paused, looking at him lovingly.

"And soon after, your brother came," she sipped, pausing enough to let him digest what she was saying.

. . .

"It is a big change - a life of duty".

Hupert was starting to grasp the parallel between his mother and Maggie.

"You don't approve", he said sadly, "...of me .... and Maggie", anxiously awaiting her response.

"Oh no, my child. I want to see you happy," she answered.

He nodded.

"King and Queens have had mistresses and lovers for centuries. But they've always known what came first", she continued.

"Gan-Gan!!!" Hupert was shocked.

"The Kingdom and the people come first, and one must do whatever is necessary to protect them." Queen Cecilia looked deeply into his eyes.

"I did what I had to", she said as she stood up and walked toward her antiqued lacquered French desk.

. . .

She paused, wondering if she was doing the right thing. She opened the drawer and took out a small stack of letters closely kept together by a red ribbon.

"Here", Queen Cecilia said as she handed them over. "I hope you will find what you are seeking". She thought he had a right to know, so long had passed.

King Albert was still in despair, the world's weight on his shoulders.

"How could you, father?" Albert asked in anger. "How could you hide this from me?"

"Son, try to understand", King Maximilian said, attempting an explanation.

"What is there to understand?" Albert continued. "Hupert was at the wheel, and you and Commander Philips have been hiding this secret for more than twenty years", now shouting.

"Commander Philips was following my orders. I had just lost your mother and almost lost your brother. It would have destroyed him to know at that time", he pleaded, "And it would have destroyed the two of you. You needed each other."

· · ·

Albert was still angry. "You could have told me later".

"For what reason, if not causing a wedge between the two of you?" King Maximilian asked. "Family is all that matters."

"And where you going to tell me about *maman?* The paternity ..." Albert persisted.

"Never, if I could help it", he replied with a tear in his eye.

"She betrayed you; he is not your son. He is not ...."

"Don't you dare! Don't you dare say it!" he snarled. "Sometimes love hurts Albert!"

"I loved her and I forgave her. Family and the Kingdom is all that matters".

"Yes, and now the Kingdom is at risk ...".

3

THE 'LOST' LETTERS

Maggie had been pacing the length and depth of the Hupert's quarters, waiting for him to return. She had desperately wanted to be part of the conversation. Still, he had been adamant she could not attend the meeting.

It was a closed family meeting; not even Albert's wife, Queen Violet, would be in attendance. She felt better about that particular, but still ...

Hours went by, and no sign of Hupert.

After leaving Queen Cecilia , he was unsure what to do; the stack of letters was burning a hole in his hands. Hupert was dying to read them; he had so many unanswered questions. He knew he should go back to Maggie; she must be worried sick. But he couldn't.

· · ·

He needed solitude.

When he was little, he always hid in his father's privy garden when he wanted to be alone. It was one of his favourite places.

There, he started reading ... he felt sick: his mother and her lover, their forbidden love.

"My darling,

Don't be afraid of how much I want you. I will protect you with my love and shield you with kisses and caresses.

I want to descend in all the joys of the flesh with you so that you faint. I want you to be amazed by me and admit that you have never dreamed of such a love possible ...

And then, when you are old, I want you to remember and tremble with delight when you think of me.

Yours always".

Hupert gasped. It's not what you want to read about your mother.

"My darling, my love",

---

she replied in another letter.

"You have shattered my resistance.

There are not enough words to tell you what I feel.

It's a feeling I only get every time you're near, and I fear waking up from this dream.

In your arms is where I want to be. Forever".

"Oh God," Hupert was sweating.

"Nothing ever feels so right as when you hold me tight with your arms wrapped around me.

Your rose".

Then another letter from 'Him'.

"You have raised new hope and fun in me, and I love you.

All this madness I asked of you, I know there is confusion in your silence — but there are no actual words to describe my great love.

I miss you, my love, why are you silent?

Always yours, here waiting."

He thought she stopped writing ...

"I nearly forgot what love was like until I met you.

Your first touch, first kiss, the first time you held me close. You make me feel like I can fly again.

Why won't you write? I have the most precious jewel with me, yours".

She thought he stopped writing. "The most precious jewel", he repeated.

"Last night, I dreamed about you; I do not know what occurred precisely. What I do know is that we kept fusing into one another. I was you. You were me.

Then, we caught fire. I remember I was extinguishing the fire with my shirt. But you were different, a shadow, as sketched with chalk, and you were lifeless, fading away from me.

Please don't leave me, my darling rose. I am nothing without you."

Hupert continued, more letters ...

"My love,

In your arms, I am at ease; the world fades; it is only you and I, and nothing else matters.

In your arms, I am free; I can be more than I ever thought imaginable.

Soon I won't be able to hide it. Where are you?"

"I did what I had to do", his grandmother had told him.

"The Kingdom and the people come first, and one must do whatever is necessary to protect them."

And now it was him putting the Kingdom at risk, once again.

4

THE SECRET

Hupert was shaking. His mother was ready to leave the King for her lover. Either, however, thought the other had changed their mind and stopped writing.

His mother would have sacrificed everything. And then, when she thought he abandoned her, she returned to the fold and dedicated her life to the Kingdom and charities: children, abandoned mothers, broken families. Everyone thought she was a saint for her tireless work and adored her.

"It was her atonement. For me", Hupert cried.

Anger, resentment, nausea, shame and frustration mixed in a dangerous cocktail.

• • •

"Was she ever happy? Did she ever really love the King?" questions that no one could ever answer.

"Father loved her; he forgave her".

Still he could not blame her. She led from the heart.

"But who was he, my 'real' father?" Hupert was also wondering. "Mother called him 'Prince'; he signed with a 'G'".

He looked at the list of all the royals around his father's age.

"Now understand why. Now I know", Hupert said when he realised.

The feud finally made sense. He had to be sure.

"I want to meet my biological father", Hupert blurted out at King Maximilian.

"I was waiting for that, Son", King Maximilian said.
    Hupert had the letters in his hand.

"I see", he said resigned.

. . .

"Is it King George III of Saint Moncito?" Hupert asked, seeking confirmation of his suspicions.

"Yes," the King replied with a long sigh.

"Is that what you two …?" And before Hupert could finish his sentence.

"Yes."

"Does he know I am his Son?".

"Yes, he does now". King Maximilian was overtaken by emotion "He wants to meet you".

"You could be King one day", and as he said it, he sat down exhausted.

"King?"

"You are the one and only heir to the Kingdom of Saint Moncito, should you wish to be".

"Wish to be?"Hupert asked.

. . .

"Son, for you to become first in line to that throne, King George would need to recognise you as his son and successor".

"But, everyone would know ..." Hupert commented.

"Yes, everyone would know".

5

FOR KING AND COUNTRY

Maggie had tried to distract herself by sending emails and checking her social media.

"Maggie", Hupert called as he could not see her.

"Hi, baby", she replied with a smile. "How did it go?" she went on anxiously curious.

"Not now, baby. I need a hug. I need a long big hug", his eyes red and swollen.

He kissed her slowly and deeply, his hands holding her tight. "I need you", licking her lips. "I need you".

Maggie loved seeing glimpses of his vulnerability behind his alpha male demeanour.

. . .

"I am here, baby—just the two of us," kissing him back voraciously, unbuttoning his shirt.

She could feel him getting harder and swayed her body over his.

"Oh God, baby", being with her was the cure he needed.

He ripped her clothes off.

"Baby, they are designer", she moaned.

"Who cares? I'll buy you some more", he replied. "I want you to sit on me and fuck me like this is my last day on earth", taking his trousers off as quickly as possible.

He lay down, his penis hard and waiting to feel her warm pussy slide in.

She made him wait, slowly removing the remaining garments. One by one. Swaying her hips, licking her lips.

"Oh God, you are torturing me," he got up and pushed her down on the bed, moving her panties to the side to enter her.

. . .

He went fast and hard, "Baby, slow down; it's hurting me", Maggie moaned.

"Let go, you know you love it". Hupert, in charge, throbbing on her.

Maggie was losing control, the pain and pleasure too strong to bear.

He *pound pound pounded* and then withdrew to finish her off with his tongue.

In a state of heightened sexual arousal, Maggie squirted all over his face.

They lay in bed in silence for a while, exhausted.

Time went by.

Hupert got up, butt naked and reached for the letters in his trousers pocket.

"Here", handing them to Maggie.

. . .

She slowly started reading, feeling his pain from every sigh. The tragic accident had elevated her to pseudo-sainthood in everyone's eyes, in his eyes, and now, now, she had fallen.

"She wanted to leave," he said.

Maggie nodded.

"Where did you find these?" holding the letters.

"My grandmother had them; she pretty much told me she was responsible for stopping the affair. 'I did what I had to do', she said".

"And now I have to make the same choice, " Hupert said.

"The Treaty between Moldof and Monois is very real; it was not just vain talking by Victoria. They can veto marriages in Monois if they choose to".

Maggie was now shivering.

"What happens if you don't comply?" she asked, fearful.

"The Kingdom could loose its sovereignty or have too

relinquish a considerable part of the territory", he answered.

She clasped her hands on her mouth. The gravity of the situation

"Baby, I couldn't ... I cannot," Maggie was shaking, "be responsible for that ... I ..."

"Stop, I love you", Hupert said.

"I .. can't, we can't do that to your family, your people. Think about your people".

"I know, but I can't Maggie. I love you too much".

"History is repeating itself", Hupert thought. And, like his mother, he would need to choose between love or King and country. And he was his mother's son.

6

———

A TINY LITTLE CLAUSE

Maggie and Hupert couldn't endure leaving each other sight and spent the next few days making love incessantly, crying most of the time.

"When are you going to tell your father and the King?" Maggie asked.

"I need more time," Hupert replied; the thought of letting Maggie go was unbearable.

"I want to meet my father", he then blurted out.

"King Maximilian?" she asked.

"No. My mother's lover, King George III of Saint Moncito", Hupert replied.

. . .

Knock knock

"Come in", King Albert responded.

"Your Royal Highness", Sir Clinton addressed him as he entered the room.

"I have reviewed the Treaty with the lawyers, Sir", the private secretary proceeded. King Albert trusted him with his life.

"There is an obscure clause in the appendixes of the Treaty that could help", he continued.

King Albert looked hopeful.

"The clause allows the party in breach to compensate financially instead of relinquishing territories."

"How much?" the King asked.

"The figure is a percentage of the worth of the territories at the time of the breach", Sir Clinton replied. "This much, Your Majesty", showing the figure.

. . .

King Albert nodded. "That much!
Anything else?"

"I found another document, less straightforward", the secretary responded.

"It involves the Kingdom of Saint Moncito and an agreement between Saint Moncito, Moldof and Monois; it would supersede Clause 23d of the 1848 Treary with Moldof".

The royal secretary held over the document from the lawyer. "Here, Sir, the part highlighted in yellow", pointing.

"Thank you, Sir Clinton", King Albert replied. "It's time for another family meeting".

Queen Cecilia had wondered for days if she had done the right thing. She knew it was too painful for her son to reveal the name of his wife's lover. Or to answer anymore questions. The relationship between the two cousins had ben strained ever since.

In her heart though, she knew, Hupert had the right to know. Her beloved grandson. She just hoped he would make the right decision.

The family reunited again; they hadn't spoken since the last meeting.

. . .

King Albert was still angry , but his priorities were protecting the kingdom and the reputation of his family and mother. He started to speak:

"Dear all,
    our lawyers have been looking in our predicament and it appears that there is a clause which allows us to compensate financially instead of relinquishing territories".

"How wonderful!" Queen Cecilia said enthusiastically.

"What is the 'but'?" King Maximilian asked.

"The figure is exorbitant and we cannot use public funds unless we want people to know why we did", he answered.

King Albert circulated the document with the figure.

"I have still Mother's inheritance," Hupert commented.
    "So have I" King Albert nodded.

"Doesn't the King of Moldof need to agree though?" Queen Cecilia asked.

"He does. However Moldof's government has been under severe pressure to boost its cash flow due to on going bad investments and their infrastructures are in great need of repair", he replied.

"We could also use something else", King Albert added, and he circulated the agreement between Saint Moncito, Moldof and Monois. "Read the part highlighted in yellow".

"We just need King George to side with us".

"I'll meet with him", Hupert said.
Everyone agreed.

Hupert was nervous and excited, he had so many questions about his mother, their story but when they finally met, he froze.

"Son", King George said, "You are the spitting image of your mother , more and more, every day that goes by", his arms were open, waiting.

Hupert reluctantly moved forward. He felt as he was betraying his Father.

They hugged.

"I have so many questions to ask you", Hupert said.

· · ·

"I know", King George answered. "This girl, do you love her?" He then asked.

"With all my heart. I'd give up anything for her".

"Very well".

7

______

THE LOST KINGDOM

After a few weeks, the two Royal Palaces released a statement in short succession from each other.

Twitter @HRHKingGeorgeIII_CommunicationOffice

From His Royal Highness King George III

______

The succession to the throne of Saint Moncito is regulated through descent and in line with the Treaty of Utrastt (2012). The order of succession is the sequence of members of the Royal Family in the order in which they stand in line to the throne.

King George III of Saint Moncito, given his declining health and lack of progeny, aims to secure the line of his succession to ensure the stability and continuity of the Kingdom.

Therefore, His Majesty has offered the succession of the throne to his first cousin once-removed, His Royal Highness Prince Hupert of Monois.

Prince Hupert of Monois and Saint Moncito will now reside with his fiancee in Rottanham Cottage at Saint Moncito Palace.

As much as King George wanted to recognise him publicly, this was best for every one concerned.

Twitter @HMMaximilianIII_CommunicationOffice

From HM King Maximilian III

His Royal Highness Prince Hupert of Monois and Ms Margaret Meddle are engaged to be married.

His Majesty, King Maximilian, is delighted to announce the engagement of Prince Hupert to Ms Margaret Meddle.

The wedding will take place in Spring 2024. The particulars of the wedding day will be announced closer to the time in due course.

His Royal Highness and Ms. Meddle became engaged in Monois earlier this month. Prince Hupert has informed His

Majesty, King Albert, and other close members of his family. Prince Hupert has also sought and received the blessing of Ms. Meddle's parents.

The couple will live in Rottanham Cottage at Saint Moncito Palace following His Royal Highness appointment as successor to the throne of Saint Moncito.

It was official: they were engaged to be married. Victoria had been beaten and a tragedy averted.

The time had now come for Maggie to choose between the love of her life and her passion project turned into dream career.

He was ready to sacrifice it all for her. One day she would be Queen now, her blog and worldwide travelling had to stop.

The Veuve had grown exponentially from a lifestyle blog, posting her favourite recipes, fun photos, and innermost thoughts, to an authority on all things royals and a large community of like-minded people.

She had named it after her favourite champagne, Veuve Cliquot.

Now, it was all coming to an end.

• • •

Tears started falling down her cheeks as she was writing. Sadness and joy.

"Farewell, Darlings",

she started writing.

"After some incredible years of this experience with you, it's time to say au revoir to The Veuve, "

tears streaming down.

"What began as a passion project and dream matured into a fantastic and supportive community. You've made each day of this journey filled with happiness. Keep finding those sparkling Veuve moments and, whatever you want, take chances.

She paused.

"Never forget that you more than enough - you are the Queen/King of your reality. Be what you want to see.

Thank you. With love.

M xx"

It was a long, heartfelt decision, but it had to be done. The media scrutiny would only intensify with the wedding to Hupert.

Any self-written blog would only exacerbate attention and be exploited, fuelling false speculation about her personal life with the prince.

She looked at the note one more time. Send. It was done.

"Goodbye Veuve, Hello Saint Moncito".

EPILOGUE

M*aggie*

As I enter the majestic grandeur of the cathedral, the intricate details of the ornate walls and the vibrant hues of the stained-glass windows captivate my senses. The lingering scent of incense adds a touch of solemnity to the air as Hupert kneels before the Archbishop of Saint Moncito, his hand resting on the ancient leather-bound book of coronation oaths.

My heart swells with pride and love at the sight of my husband, soon to be crowned King Hupert I. Five years ago, I wouldn't have believed we'd come this far, weathering the trials and tribulations that accompanied our whirlwind romance. But here we are now, preparing to embark on this new chapter of our lives together—side by side, as King and Queen Consort.

. . .

My eyes drift to our son, little George Hupert Maximilian, sleeping peacefully in his nurse's arms, oblivious to the momentous occasion. My heart clenched with joy at the thought of all the possibilities before him as a royal heir.

Tears of happiness brim in my eyes as I remember the sacrifices my husband was prepared to make for our love. But through it all, he'd never wavered in his devotion to me or our relationship. And now, here we stand, surrounded by friends and family who have come to accept our love story for what it was—a fairy tale for the modern age.

Hupert

I kneel before the Archbishop, my eyes fixed on Maggie's face as she stands beside me. Her beauty steals my breath away, and I can hardly believe this day has finally arrived. Gone are the days I felt like a mere backup plan for the Monoisian throne. Today, as I prepare to take the oath of office as King of Saint Moncito, I am filled with a sense of purpose and fulfilment like never before.

My love for Maggie burns brighter than ever, just as it did when we reunited after twenty years apart. Fate brought us back together, and now she is my everything. Without her, I would still be living in my brother's shadow and merely going through the motions of life. But Maggie has changed all of that, bringing light into every dark corner of my exis-tence and making me feel truly alive.

· · ·

As I rise to my feet with the heavy St. Edward's Crown atop my head, I silently vow to be the kind of king that Maggie deserves—fair, just, and dedicated to serving the people of Saint Moncito above all else. Together, we will usher in a new golden age for our adopted country—a time defined by love, understanding, and compassion.

With the coronation ceremony complete, I turn to Maggie and offer my hand. "Your Highness," I say formally before flashing her a mischievous grin that only she can see. "Shall we consummate our union?"

Maggie blushes deeply but takes my hand without hesitation as we lead our guests back to the Palace for the celebrations. She knows our love scene will have to wait until later that evening when we can steal a few precious moments alone together. But when we do, it will be worth the wait.

GET YOUR FREE EBOOK

Sign up the Laura (L.A.) Mariani mailing list for a FREE steamy romance.

You'll be the first to hear about new releases, exclusive offers, bonus content and all Laura's news. You can even email her back. She loves chatting with her readers!

To claim your free ebook visit:
https://laura-mariani-author.ck.page/freeshortstory

AUTHOR'S NOTE

Thank you so much for reading *A Royal Romance Trilogy*.

I hope you enjoyed the stories. A review would be much appreciated as it helps other readers discover the story.

Thanks.

Laura xx

Places in the book

I have set the story in real places like Eton and Windsor, New York City and the fictional kingdom of *Moinos, Moldof* and *Saint Moncito*.

Bibliography

I read a lot as part of my research. Some of the references include:

The 5 Most Important Treaties in World History
by Akhilesh Pillalamarri - The National Interest
List of Treaties - **Wikipedia**
List of Treaties - **Britannica**

You can see the places/mentions below - find out more
about them or perhaps go and visit:

Gilbey's Bar, Restaurant and Townhouse
Eton
Eton college
Windsor Castle

DISCLAIMER

A Royal Romance Trilogy is a work of fiction.

With the exception of public places, any resemblance to persons living or dead is coincidental. Space and time have been rearranged to suit the convenience of the book, memory has its own story to tell.

The opinions expressed are those of the characters and should not be confused with the author's.

ABOUT THE AUTHOR

Laura Alexandra (L.A.) Mariani is a best selling author of Short & Steamy Romance | Where Alpha Males Meet Fierce Heroines for Sweet Endings, your go-to author for captivating romance tales that will sweep you off your feet and keep you on the edge of your seat!

When Laura is not weaving stories of love, desire and suspense, you'll find her exploring the vibrant streets of London, drawing inspiration from its hidden corners and bustling markets, or strolling through the charming streets of Paris, savoring street food in Rome, or relaxing on a sun-kissed beach in Bali, her journeys fuelling her creativity and infuse her stories with wanderlust.

You can also follow her on

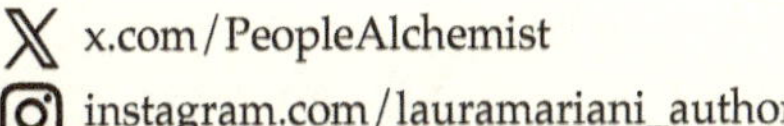

x.com/PeopleAlchemist
instagram.com/lauramariani_author